D1722685

The "C" Seven Club

The "C" Seven Club

If you can dream it!

Sharla Hogue

Published by Tablo

The "C" Seven Club

Welcome to the "C "Seven Club. Once you read this book you will never be the same. To become a member in this group you must take the secret oath. Everyone in this group understands how important their thoughts are. They might be young but they know a secret, one that some adults don't believe. The secret lies hidden in our body's light energy that uses your imagination to make things happen. With their superpower the members create a fantasy world where all their dreams come true, anything is possible, anything.

To become a full fledged member in this club there are three key rules:

- you must believe that you have the power to make things happen.
- you must be able to create dreams in your imagination.
- you must learn how to "feel" what is happening in your dreams before it happens in the real world.

So when dreams come true in the real world, our members have already felt the excitement the joy and happiness of their dreams come true. Lastly you must trust that no matter how long it takes, it will happen, your dream or something better will come your way. Once you Pass your "C" Seven requirements you will be asked to share your secret with others.

Day after day our members experience that light energy that works with their imagination

In this book you will read a story about Taylor who is one of our members in the "C" Seven Club. See what happens when he discovers his superpowers.

Gurwrinkles

Gwurk

Gurwrinkle's, (Gwurks for short) are everywhere; they can be in your house, at school, in grocery stores, at a friends homes, at hockey arenas, and swimming pools, even at birthday parties. Some Gwurks show up at your parents work, in Dr. offices, at the dentist; everywhere there are people Gwurks can find their way into your space. You can usually tell a Gwurk by their faces; they have a clenched jaw, intense eye contact, furrowed brow and reddish skin. When they talk it is through their gritted teeth. If you sit with a group of them they look like they have been sucking on a jar of sour pickles. Once they enter into the room if you are not careful they can suck you into their place of unhappiness and turn your good feelings into bad ones. What the Gwurks don't know is that everyone has a superpower that they can use to block their negative energy, the bad feelings that they are throwing at you.

Gwurk

Gurwrinkle

Gwurk

If you can Dream it...

Taylor

Taylor

Taylor is a lanky, blond hair; blue-eyed, kind, and good-looking nine-year-old boy. He lives in a lovely neighborhood in a tutor style home, with his mom and dad along with his feisty younger sister named Olivia

They have two dogs, named Murray, and Quincey who love to play outside and go on long runs with the family whenever they get a chance.

Quincey and Murray

Taylor is just like most nine year olds; he goes to school, loves his family, his dogs and playing sports. He says he would prefer that his sister would have been a brother because well, she's a girl and at nine years old Taylor does not want to hang out with any girls, especially one that he has to live with all the time! Secretly though he knows that Olivia is one of his biggest fans who would do anything for him and probably one day they will be best friends, just not now.

Olivia

Taylor and Olivia with their mom and dad

Taylor loves any sports, and would love to be a profession athlete one day but his absolute favourite pastime is to plays hockey with his cousin Henry who lives a couple of blocks away.

Noah and Henry

Future Hockey Star

Although Taylor is only nine-years-old he knows a secret that many other people don't know, even most adults. This secret gives him superpowers. Powers that help him every day, so much so that Taylor can't even imagine what his life would be like without these powers. Taylor knows that he can do or have anything he wants to. He knows that if he wants more friends at school, he can have that. He knows if he wants to be better at sports, he can do that. He knows that if he wants to grow up to be a doctor, a football player, or a hockey star he can do that. He knows if he wanted to be a movie star, who drives a red Ferrari,

Noah future car

a famous author or singer, if he wanted to play guitar, the trombone or the piano he could do that. With his superpower he can have anything or be anything he puts his mind to.

A great piano to learn on

Taylor found out about his secret powers by accident when he was six years old. You see Taylor used to be a worrywart, he would worry in the mornings, that he would be late for school, he would worry just before lunch that he would not like his lunch, he would worry that when he got home he would not be able to play outside, Noah worried all the time. Worry, worry, worry about everything and anything. This particular day was no different, he had spent all night working on an assignment his teacher, Mrs. MacInnis, gave him and he was super proud of his work but worried that maybe he should have used different colors, that his papers would get wrinkled before he could hand them in or worse yet, what if he dropped the papers in a big muddy pool of water on his way to school and it ruined his work??

When he stepped out of his house it was a windy afternoon

Gwurk watching

Assignment in the wind

Taylor had his homework assignment in his hand. He thought he could feel someone looking at him, but when he looked around there was no one there. Taylor could not shake the feeling that he was not alone, something was watching him and next thing he knew his homework papers got caught in the wind and whirled around in front of him.

Then they whirled to the right of him spinning in all different directions, left, right, back and forth, up and down and then whirled right in front of his face. No matter how hard he tried he could not catch those papers, they were just out of his reach until they flew way over his head and then totally out of sight.

"Oh no" Taylor thought "what am I going to do? I worked so hard on that homework and I really want Mrs. MacInnis to see it." That is when it first happened. He did not know it yet but his superpowers, his light energy was waiting for him to discover what he could do. A power force that is with him all the time, one he can pull from at anytime in anyplace. He thought about the homework papers and pictured them in his mind and how much he wanted to bring them into school to show them off.

He closed his eyes and that is when it happened, he entered a different place through a secret energy opening? It was like he was in the same place but everything was totally different. He felt light, happy and absolutely worry free. Colors were more vivid; sounds were extra beautiful even the air that filled his lungs felt fresher, everything was the same but different. He focused on having those papers again, he pictured his running shoe with the papers underneath it; he imagined how he would just bend over and pick them up and what that would feel like. He could actually feel and see the papers back in his hand. The picture in his mind was so vivid and real, his finger clutched tightly to the white paper with his coloring masterpiece on it. His whole body and mind could feel and sense the delightful feeling of getting those papers back. He was not just thinking it would happen anymore he knew it would. He pictured walking into his classroom with the homework in his hand and as he was handing them over to his teacher Mrs. MacInnis.

Mrs. MacInnis

He pictured the smile on Mrs. MacInnis face and how proud he would feel handing over his particular assignments. A big smile came to his face as he felt how proud he was when Mrs. MacInnis told him that" this is one of the best coloring projects" she had ever seen. He felt like he was already at school, but everything was the same but so different, different in a way that just made him feel so peaceful and calm and for once in a very long time he was not worried about anything. In his mind he had already given Mrs. MacInnis the homework, and best of all he could actually feel that overwhelming sensation of how proud he was handing over that assignment. Taylor almost forgot where he was, he was so immersed in his imagination. When he opened his eyes, everything was back to how it was before he went into that secret place in his imagination he looked down and there was his homework under the toe of his right shoe.

Just like he pictured it his assignment under his shoe

Assignment back in his hands

"Wow!" Taylor said, as he bent over and picked up the homework and ran as fast as he could to school. This time Taylor was holding on to his homework papers super tight, he was not going to lose them again!

All the way to school he had this gut feeling like he had already done this before, everything was familiar, running down the street, the wind was still blowing but Taylor was enjoying the cool breeze on his face. The trees had beautiful birds chirping different songs from their branches and he had the assignment clutched tightly in his hand. He was not worried about anything, he knew it was going to be a great day because he had already pictured it happening. As he walked into the classroom he felt butterflies in his stomach and his excitement grew because he was just about to hand in the best assignment ever.

It was just like he pictured in his mind. Mrs. MacInnis was at the front of the classroom writing something on the black board,

Mrs. MacInnis at the blackboard

she turned around as Taylor walked up to the front of the classroom he handed her his homework, and then just how he imagined her smiling and saying "Taylor, this is one of the best coloring projects I have ever seen!" He felt so proud, and realized as he walked back to his desk that it happened just as he had pictured it in his mind.

That was over three years ago and since then Taylor uses his powers all the time. He goes to that positive wonderful place in his imagination, sometimes several times a day where everything is just a little brighter, happier, worry free and full of love and happiness. He realizes how important his thinking is, that his thoughts actually become things. He is very careful to focus on and think about as many good things as possible.

Just another dream

Off to another adventure.

His favourite time now is bedtime, just before he falls asleep where he can let his imagination run away with him to all the different places and things that he wants. He knows if he can dream it - He can have it! His favorite dream at the moment is becoming an ornithologists, but that is another story…

The C Seven Pledge

I believe that:

My thoughts are powerful.

My mind is my superpower - I will use my superpowers to help me and help other people.

The stories I invent in my imagination change my world.

I know that no matter where I am my light energy surrounds me.

Inside of me is a super power to create my dreams and my perfect life.

Now that I understand this, life will never be the same.

Never-ever-ever!!

I will use my imagination to make the world a better place.

I pledge to be a "C "Seven forever!

The Original "C" Seven Members

The original kids from the C Seven Club

CPSIA information can be obtained
at www.ICGtesting.com
Printed in the USA
BVHW021927090721
611450BV00029B/686/J

9 781649 697424